by Theo. LeSieg

Illustrated by

Roy McKie

A Bright & Early Book

RANDOM HOUSE / NEW YORK

Published in the United States by Random House, Inc., New York, and simultaneously in Canada by Random House of Canada Limited, Toronto. Manufactured in the United States of America.

This title was originally catalogued by the Library of Congress as follows: Seuss, Dr. The eye book. Illus. by Roy McKie. Random House [c1968] unp. illus. (Bright and early books for beginning beginners) Eyes see a lot of things in various shapes, colors, sizes, etc.–and here are some of the things that eyes see. 1. Eye. I. Title. PZ7.G2719Ey [E] 68-28463 ISBN 0-394-81094-5 ISBN 0-394-91094-X (lib. bdg.)

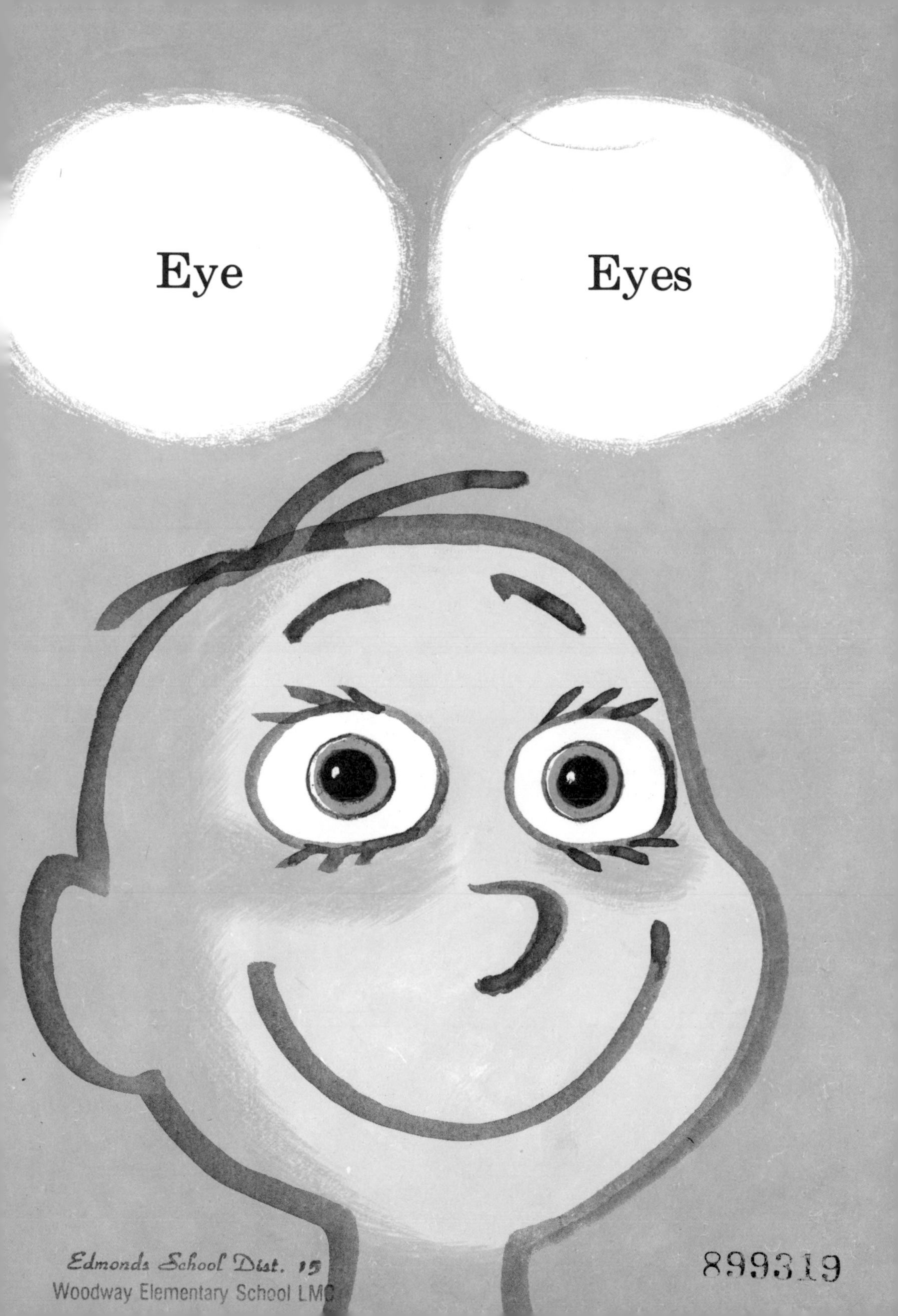
Eye
Eyes

My eyes
My eyes

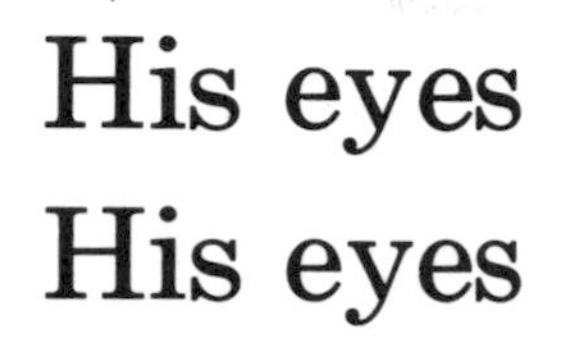

His eyes
His eyes

Wink eye
Wink eye

Pink eye Pink eye

My eyes see.

His eyes see.

I see him.

And he sees me.

Our eyes see blue.

Our eyes see red.

They see a bird.

They see a bed.

They see the sun.

They see the moon.

They see a fork

a knife

a spoon.

They see a girl.

They see a man . . .

a boy

a horse

an old tin can.

They look down holes.

They look up poles.

Our eyes see trees.

They look at clocks.

They look at bees.

They look at socks.

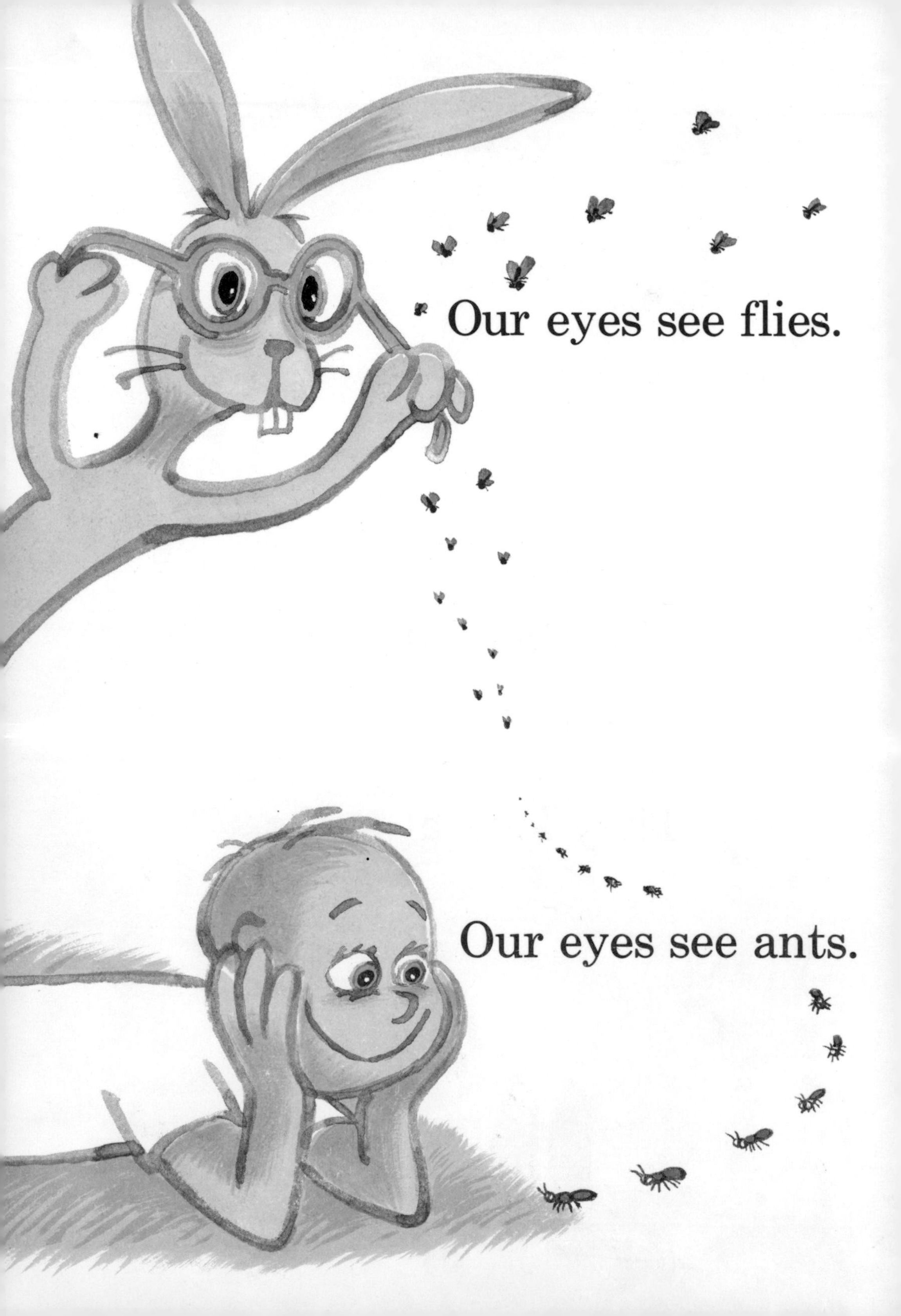

Our eyes see flies.

Our eyes see ants.

Sometimes they see
pink underpants.

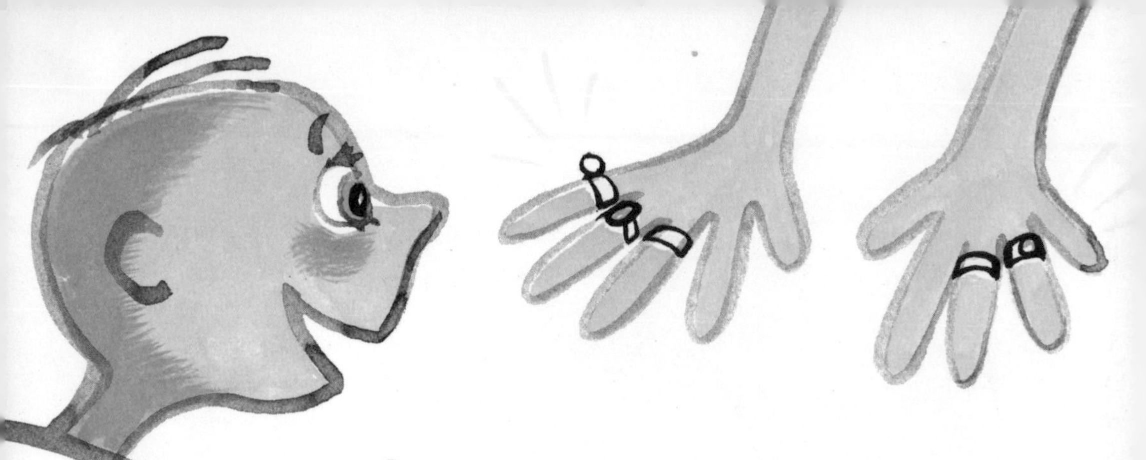

Our eyes see rings.

Our eyes see strings.

They see
so many, many things!

So many things!

Like rain

and pie . . .

and dogs

and airplanes
in the sky!

And so we say,
"Hooray for eyes!
Hooray, hooray, hooray . . .

. . . for eyes!"